THUDD

Hiya! My name Thudd. Best robot friend of Drewd. Thudd know lots of stuff about frogs and ponds. How tadpole lose tail and turn into frog. How baby bug start out like worm in pond and grow up to be flying bug. Some reasons why frogs disappearing.

Drewd like to invent stuff. Thudd help! But Drewd make lotsa mistakes. Drewd invent shrinking machine. Now Drewd small as bug. Drewd invent flying machine to visit frog pond. Lots of danger! Frogs eat bugs! Will frogs eat Drewd? Want to find out? Turn page, please!

Get lost with
Andrew, Judy, and Thudd
in all their exciting adventures!

ANDREW LOST

18

WITH THE FROGS

BY J. C. GREENBURG

ILLUSTRATED
BY JAN GERARDI

A STEPPING STONE BOOK™

Random House 🏠 New York

*To Dan, Zack, and the real Andrew,
with a galaxy of love.
To the children who read these books: I wish
you wonderful questions. Questions are
telescopes into the universe!
—J.C.G.*

*To Cathy Goldsmith, with many thanks.
—J.G.*

Text copyright © 2008 by J. C. Greenburg
Illustrations copyright © 2008 by Jan Gerardi

All rights reserved. Published in the United States by Random House Children's Books, a division of Random House, Inc., New York.

Random House and colophon are registered trademarks and A Stepping Stone Book and colophon are trademarks of Random House, Inc. Andrew Lost is a trademark of J. C. Greenburg.

Visit us on the Web!
www.randomhouse.com/kids/AndrewLost
www.AndrewLost.com

Educators and librarians, for a variety of teaching tools, visit us at www.randomhouse.com/teachers

Library of Congress Cataloging-in-Publication Data
Greenburg, J. C. (Judith C.)
With the frogs / by J. C. Greenburg ; illustrated by Jan Gerardi. — 1st ed.
    p.   cm. — (Andrew Lost ; 18) "A Stepping Stone Book."
Summary: Still reduced to the size of insects, Andrew, Judy, and the robot Thudd go to a pond, where they encounter dragonflies, moss animals, and fierce larvae in an attempt to learn why frogs are disappearing throughout the world.
ISBN 978-0-375-84668-7 (trade) — ISBN 978-0-375-94668-4 (lib. bdg.)
[1. Ponds—Fiction. 2. Pond animals—Fiction. 3. Insects—Fiction. 4. Size—Fiction. 5. Cousins—Fiction.] I. Gerardi, Jan, ill. II. Title.
PZ7.G82785Wj 2008   [Fic]—dc22   2007044402

Printed in the United States of America
10 9 8 7 6 5 4 3 2   First Edition

THUDD

CONTENTS

ANDREW'S WORLD

Andrew Dubble

Andrew is ten years old, but he's been inventing things since he was four. His inventions usually get him in trouble, like the time he accidentally took the Time-A-Tron on a trip to the beginning of the universe.

Andrew's newest invention was supposed to save the world from getting buried in garbage. Instead, it squashed Andrew and his cousin Judy down to bug size. They got hauled off to a dump, thrown up by a seagull, carried off to a rain forest, and stuck inside their uncle Al!

Now Andrew is flying off to a frog pond to investigate why frogs are disappearing all over the world. But will Andrew be the one who's disappearing?

Judy Dubble

Judy is Andrew's thirteen-year-old cousin. She's been snuffled into a dog's nose, pooped out of a whale, and had her pajamas chewed by a Tyrannosaurus—all because of Andrew. Judy had promised herself that she'd never let Andrew talk her into another stupid adventure again. But then she got hungry. . . .

Thudd

The **H**andy **U**ltra-**D**igital **D**etective. Thudd is a super-smart robot and Andrew's best friend. He has helped save Andrew and Judy from the exploding sun, the giant squid, and the really weird stuff inside

Uncle Al. Now can he protect his buddies from the jaws of a water tiger?

The Goa Constrictor

This giant fake snake is Andrew's newest invention. *Goa* is sort of short for **G**arbage **Go**es **A**way. The Goa is supposed to keep the world from getting buried in garbage by squashing rotting vegetables, green meat, and dirty diapers down to teensy-weensy specks. Unfortunately for Andrew and Judy, the Goa doesn't just shrink garbage. In two minutes and one stinky burp, the Goa can shrink anything—and anyone!

At first the Goa shrank Andrew and Judy to the size of beetles. But since then, they've been changing size more often than some people change their underwear!

GOTTA WEAR YOUR WANNABEE

"Ergh!" grunted ant-sized Andrew Dubble. Andrew, wearing a furry black-and-yellow-striped jumpsuit, was on a ledge outside a kitchen window.

His arms were covered by black metal tubes, jointed at the elbows. He was struggling to get his legs into pants made from the same tubes.

"You're not supposed to be outside, Bug-Brain," came a voice from the window sill behind him. "And what's with that *stupid* outfit?"

It was Andrew's thirteen-year-old cousin, Judy. Judy was ant-sized, too.

"I'm dragging you back inside," she said as she climbed through a hole in the screen and onto the ledge.

Andrew stood up stiffly in his metal pants. "I figured that since we're bug-sized, we need some bug advantages," he said. "So I made us these suits. They're called Wannabees."

Judy rolled her eyes. "Bug *advantages*!" she said. "I don't want anything that bugs have! I just want what humans have—like being human size!"

A few weeks ago, Andrew was working on his latest invention, the Goa, short for **G**arbage **Go**es **A**way. The Goa was supposed to squash garbage down to the size of specks. Andrew did shrink some apple cores and stinky cheese, but he also accidentally shrank himself and Judy down to bug size.

"Uncle Al is working on getting us big again," said Andrew. "But we're so small that we need protection right now. We're so soft, we could get crushed or eaten if something big comes along. Bugs are little, too, and they've got lots of ways to protect themselves."

meep . . . "Hit Drewd!" came a squeaky voice from a pocket in Andrew's Wannabee.

It was Andrew's little silver robot and pocket-sized best friend, Thudd.

"That's the best idea I've heard since we got shrunk," said Judy. She made a fist and punched Andrew hard in the chest.

"Ooof!" she said, rubbing her hand. "It's like you've got a hard shell!"

"Super-duper pooper-scooper!" said Andrew. "Our skeletons are on the inside. But all insects and spiders have their skeletons on the outside, like this."

meep . . . "Called exoskeleton," said Thudd. "*Exo* mean 'outside.'"

Andrew nodded. "If you fall from a high place when you're wearing the Wannabee, you won't get hurt. If something tries to bite you, you'll be hard to chew."

He pulled the hood of the Wannabee over his head.

Andrew clomped over to a peanut shell on the window sill. He reached in and pulled out a Wannabee like the one he was wearing. He held it out to Judy.

"This one's for you," he said. "Try it on. I think it's your size."

"You've got to be kidding!" said Judy. "It looks *so* uncomfortable. Besides, every one of your stupid inventions has gotten us in trouble. If we just stay in the house, we won't need this junk."

Andrew shook his head. "We can't just hang around the house," he said. "We've got to help Uncle Al save the frogs."

Uncle Al had rescued Andrew and Judy from jungles and deserts—and even from inside himself! He had also invented Thudd.

Now he was trying to figure out why frogs were disappearing all over the world.

Judy rolled her eyes. "Ever since Uncle Al told us about the disappearing frogs, that's *all* you think about," she said.

"Some frogs have even gone extinct," said Andrew. "Uncle Al and the frogs need our help. There's a frog pond just beyond this yard. We've got to go there and see what we can find out."

"Right," said Judy. "At our size, it will take us a year to get to that pond."

"No it won't," said Andrew.

Andrew reached into a pocket and pulled out a tiny black remote control. He pressed some of its buttons.

Suddenly a dead leaf at the end of the window ledge fluttered. It lifted. Beneath it was an odd flying machine. At the top was a pair of large, buggy-looking wings that had been wired together. Beneath the wings were two little seats, and under them, three wheels.

"Cheese Louise!" said Judy. "What is *that*?"

Andrew smiled and cocked his head. "It's the GNAT," he said. "GNAT is short for **G**lobal **N**avigation **a**nd **T**ransportation.

"I made it from a pair of dragonfly wings I found in the garden and stuff in Uncle Al's workshop."

"Global!" said Judy. "That stupid-looking thing wouldn't get you from here to the kitchen sink."

"You wanna bet?" said Andrew. "I'll bet you the last crumb of Uncle Al's super-delicious fudge. I've got it in my pocket."

"Hmmmm . . . ," Judy pondered. "I'm *so* hungry. Okay."

Andrew pressed more buttons on the re-mote.

Whrrrrrrrrrrr . . .

The GNAT's wings fluttered slowly at first, then faster, then so fast that they seemed to disappear.

Whirring softly, the GNAT lifted a couple of inches off the window sill and set itself down in front of Andrew.

Andrew packed Judy's Wannabee gear in a box beneath the GNAT's seats. "You'll want your Wannabee later," he said.

"Fat chance," said Judy.

Andrew got into the left-hand seat and fastened his seat belt. He patted the seat next to him. Judy climbed in and pulled her seat belt across her lap.

"Wowzers schnauzers!" said Andrew. "Now I'll be able to test the GNAT."

"*What!*" said Judy. "You haven't tested this stupid thing?"

"You saw that it flies," said Andrew. "But if it's carrying us, it needs a lot more power."

He pointed to a set of pedals beneath

each seat. "We both need to pedal in order to keep the engine going."

Judy's nose twitched. "I smell something funny," she said.

"Mothball flakes," said Andrew. "I put some in the pockets of our Wannabees.

"Mothballs keep all kinds of bugs away—snakes, too! Mothballs mess up their sense of smell."

Judy's face went white. "Snakes!" she yelled.

Andrew sighed and looked away. "I guess I'm just braver than you are," he said.

"No you're *not*!" said Judy, pedaling.

Andrew grinned. He started pedaling, too, but nothing happened.

"I told you so," said Judy. "Give me that fudge crumb."

"Not yet," said Andrew. "The GNAT is storing energy as we pedal. It's like winding up a toy plane."

WHRRRRRRRRR . . .

Suddenly the GNAT's wings were beating. The wind from the wings bent Andrew's antennas and blew Judy's hair over her face. The GNAT lurched from side to side like a woozy clown, then it zoomed off the window ledge and into the trees.

CRASH LANDING!

The GNAT was zigging and zagging. It was flying in circles. It was doing loop-de-loops.

"Aaaaaaaaack!" hollered Judy. "Get this thing back to the house, Bug-Brain!"

Uncle Al's yard was a blur of green. The wind whooshed against them. Leaves slapped Andrew's face.

Andrew yanked at the steering wheel, but the GNAT was out of control. He quickly pressed some buttons on the remote, but his invention seemed to have a mind of its own.

"The GNAT isn't working right," said Andrew.

"Urf!" said Judy. "I feel sick!"

"Stop pedaling," said Andrew. "The GNAT will go slower. Maybe then I'll be able to land it."

As the GNAT slowed, it flew more smoothly. Andrew could steer it now.

He glimpsed a silvery glint below. *Sunlight on water!* he thought. *It's the pond!*

The GNAT was gliding down.

WHRRRRRRRRRRR . . . came a sound like the GNAT, but louder. At first all Andrew could see was a bright streak rushing at them. Then it turned and shadowed them—a long, slim green body and a blur of wings.

meep . . . "Dragonfly!" squeaked Thudd. "Fierce hunter! Eat anything that move. Catch prey with legs. Eat and fly!"

Andrew watched as the swift dragonfly dropped lower and kept pace with the GNAT. The insect's prickly legs looked like a spiny cage.

The GNAT jittered in the air. The dragonfly's mouth opened wide. It was so close that Andrew could look up and see inside. Two sets of jaws, one inside the other, were lined with needle-sharp teeth.

Andrew shuddered. His head would fit nicely inside those jaws.

The dragonfly dipped. The tips of its

clawed feet scratched Andrew's cheek.

Judy leaned over the side of the GNAT. "I see something that looks like a little raft below us," she said.

"I'll try to land us there," said Andrew, dodging a dragonfly foot.

Andrew nosed the GNAT down steeply and gained speed. They were going so fast, Andrew could feel the air pulling at his face.

With a jolt and a bounce, the GNAT landed on a bumpy surface and stopped.

"Woofers!" said Andrew.

He scanned the sky for the dragonfly. It was a foot above them. A smaller dragonfly was trapped in its cage-like legs! The big dragonfly began to chew on the smaller one.

"Holy moly!" said Andrew. "A cannibal dragonfly! But at least it's not eating us."

Judy looked down at the bumpy raft they had landed on. "Yikes!" she hollered. "What's going on here?"

The bumps on their landing place looked like the tops of tiny Ping-Pong balls. Some of them were popping open. Buggy little heads were waggling out!

meep . . . "Drewd and Oody land on raft of mosquito eggs!" said Thudd. "Wormy thing called larva hatch from egg."

"Eeeeuw!" hollered Judy. "We're on a *mosquito island*!"

As soon as each wriggly brown larva squirmed out of its egg, it disappeared into the pond.

RHUUMMMMM . . . RHUUMMMMM . . . RHUUMMMMM . . .

The deep sounds from somewhere in the pond made Andrew's chest rumble.

"Cheese Louise!" said Judy. "What's *that*?"

meep . . . "Bullfrogs!" squeaked Thudd.

There were other noises, too—chirps and whistles and trills. But the frog croaks were the loudest.

The air smelled like low tide and autumn leaves.

Andrew scanned the pond. Huge lily pads floated on the greenish water, and tall cattails swayed skyscraper-high above them.

On the surface of the pond, nothing was still. Long-legged water striders skittered around the mosquito raft. Their feet made little dents in the water as though it were a sheet of thin plastic. A spider many times bigger than Andrew raced along and stopped nearby.

"Wowzers schnauzers!" said Andrew. "The pond is like a skating rink for bugs!"

meep . . . "Water molecules on surface stick together tight, tight, tight!" said Thudd. "Make lotsa bonds with each other. More bonds than water below.

"Bonds make kinda skin on surface of water."

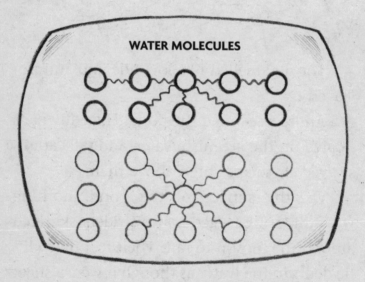

WATER MOLECULES

The spider tapped its two front legs on the water, making little ripples.

meep . . . "Spider lure prey," said Thudd.
The spider dove.

A second later, the spider came up clutching a silvery fish in its jaws. The fish was as large as the spider.

Splish! Splosh!

The fish flapped for a few seconds, then it was still.

The spider skated away with its meal.

meep . . . "Spider pour venom into prey with fangs," said Thudd. "Venom turn inside of prey into goo. Then spider suck out goo as food."

"Yuck-a-roony!" said Judy. "Spiders eating fish. Bugs eating bugs. Something could snap *us* up any minute! Let's get out of here!"

Andrew opened the box beneath their seats and pulled out Judy's Wannabee.

"Before we go anywhere," he said, "you'd better put on your Wannabee. There's a lot of weird stuff in this pond and we don't know what will happen next. The Wannabee will protect you."

meep . . . "Little bit, maybe," said Thudd.

"A little bit!" said Judy. She folded her arms over her chest and stared out at the busy pond.

"Oh, all right, give me that stupid suit," she said. "And give me the fudge crumb you promised me."

Andrew looked at Judy. "Um, I don't think so," he said. "The GNAT *did* go farther than the kitchen sink."

Judy gave Andrew her wait-till-I-get-my-hands-on-you look. "Fine," said Andrew. He reached into his pocket, pulled out the fudge crumb, and gave it to Judy.

Judy munched the crumb quickly. Then she took the Wannabee from Andrew, pulled on the fuzzy black-and-yellow-striped jump-suit, and struggled into the arm and leg tubes.

"Now we're good to go," said Andrew. "Start pedaling."

Andrew and Judy pedaled and pedaled.

Whrrrrrrrrrrr . . .

The GNAT's wings barely fluttered.

"Something's not working," said Andrew.

The GNAT teetered slowly across the mosquito raft.

Ploorp!

It splashed down in the water. The wheels sank, but the seat cushions kept the GNAT afloat.

"What's that?" said Andrew, leaning forward.

A huge white weird thing loomed in front of them.

"Aaaaaaack!" screamed Judy. "It's a floating brain!"

THE FLOATING BRAIN

meep . . . "Called moss animal!" said Thudd. "Moss animal not one animal. Is colony. Millions, millions, millions of tiny animals that live together.

"Not hurt Drewd and Oody. Moss animal eat things too small to see—germs and stuff."

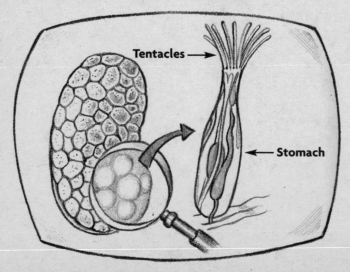

Tentacles →

← Stomach

"Gross-a-mundo!" said Judy. "Let's get out of here!"

"Pedal harder!" said Andrew.

It wasn't easy to pedal underwater, but Andrew and Judy kept at it until they were hot and sweaty. The GNAT's wings didn't even flutter.

Andrew shook his head. "Um, the GNAT isn't working," he said.

"Nothing you make ever works!" said Judy.

meep . . . "Purple-button time," said Thudd.

Thudd had three rows of three buttons on his chest. Each button glowed bright green except for the big purple button in the middle. That was the emergency button for calling Uncle Al.

Thudd pressed the big purple button. It blinked three times and went off.

Andrew pointed left. "There's a lily pad a

couple of feet away. We can paddle to it and wait for Uncle Al."

Using their hands as oars, Andrew and Judy rowed the GNAT toward the lily pad.

"Yeoouch!" cried Judy, struggling to pull her hand out of the water. "Something's got my arm! *HELP!*"

Andrew undid his seat belt and leaned over to see. Thudd crept out of Andrew's pocket, scurried over Judy's lap, and looked down.

Just below the water, an insect hung upside down. Four of its prickly legs gripped Judy's arm.

meep . . . "Backswimmer bug!" said Thudd. "Swim upside down under skin of water. Breathe by trapping air bubble in special hairs on body."

Andrew grabbed Judy's arm. "When I count to three, yank!

"One . . . two . . . three! Oooomph!"

With the yank, Judy's arm came free. But the GNAT flipped over and dumped Andrew and Judy into the water.

Eek! squeaked Thudd as he plunked into the pond.

"Blurf!" sputtered Andrew, coming up for air.

"Blaaargh!" Judy half coughed and half sneezed.

Andrew scooped Thudd up and put him

back in his pocket. "It's a good thing I gave you three coats of Protectum," said Andrew. "Your brain chips won't get soggy."

He turned to Judy. "Now aren't you glad you were wearing a Wannabee?" he asked. "That bug could have chomped your arm off."

"I'm not glad about *anything*!" said Judy.

"Come on," said Andrew. "Let's flip the GNAT over and try to fly it."

Andrew and Judy tugged and pulled, but the GNAT was bigger than they were and heavy with water.

All the while, they could hear the croaking of the frogs. Underwater, things were poking them.

One of the GNAT's wings slipped and the GNAT quickly sank.

"Uh-oh," said Andrew. "Guess we'll have to swim to the lily pad."

"Swim!" said Judy. "It's hard to even stay afloat in this stupid Wannabee!"

Andrew shrugged. "We don't have much choice," he said. "Unless you want to hitch a ride on *that*!" He pointed to a giant bug swimming toward them.

It looked like a cockroach. Its back was covered with white bumps.

"Aaaaaaack!" said Judy.

meep . . . "Giant water bug!" said Thudd. "Male giant water bug. Female water bug glue eggs onto back of male water bug. Male take care of eggs till eggs hatch.

"Giant water bug ferocious. Eat anything. Catch fish. Eat tadpoles."

Andrew treaded water quietly till the giant water bug passed by. "He doesn't seem interested in eating us," said Andrew. "Let's get to the lily pad before he changes his mind."

Andrew dog-paddled toward the lily pad. Judy pulled ahead of him. She was captain of her swim team at Benjamin Franklin Junior High.

All around them, long-legged water striders skittered over the pond. One of their feet brushed against Andrew's face.

"Oofers!" said Andrew. "These guys have fuzzy feet!"

meep . . . "Feet fuzz spread bug's weight over lotsa water," said Thudd. "Help bug stay on top."

Andrew and Judy paddled through a herd of small, round beetles spinning in circles.

"These bugs are crazy," said Andrew.

meep . . . "Called whirligig beetles," said Thudd. "Whirling make beetle hard for fish to grab."

As they got nearer to the lily pad, they swam past a giant mound of shiny beads. Each bead was the size of a pea. The beads seemed to be made of clear jelly.

Andrew got close enough to see wriggling, comma-shaped creatures inside some of the glistening beads.

"These lumps are alive!" said Andrew.

meep . . . "Frog eggs!" said Thudd. "Eggs of yellow-legged frog. Frog eggs turning into tadpoles. Tadpoles hatch out of eggs soon."

"Holy moly!" said Andrew. "The yellow-legged frogs aren't disappearing at all! When these eggs hatch, there'll be *thousands* of them in this pond!"

meep . . . "Noop! Noop! Noop!" said Thudd. "Lotsa eggs not hatch. Lotsa animals eat frog eggs and tadpoles. From one hundred frog eggs, one frog grow up, maybe."

They had almost arrived at the lily pad when a ripple shoved them away, then another and another. Two inches away, a long, centipede-like creature reared up from the pond like a cobra. Needle-like fangs curved from the sides of its round, flat head.

It looked like it had escaped from a nightmare.

WHAT A HORRIBLE BABY!

In front of the creature was a gigantic bug with pinching claws. It was a battle of fangs and claws as they slashed and struck at each other.

"Holy moly!" Andrew panted. His heart was beating like a bongo drum. "It looks like a horror movie!"

He swam against the ripples as fast as he could toward the lily pad.

meep . . . "Diving beetle larva attack adult diving beetle," said Thudd.

"Aaaaack!" screamed Judy. "What a huge, horrible baby!"

meep . . . "Larva baby bigger than adult beetle!" said Thudd.

"Adult beetle hungry and fierce, fierce, fierce!" said Thudd. "Larva baby hungry, too. And super fierce! Also called water tiger."

Judy reached the lily pad first. She climbed up onto the smooth green leaf and held a hand out to Andrew. Andrew climbed up and sat down next to Judy.

"Ugh!" said Judy, dragging her hair back from her face. "I used to think of ponds as peaceful places. I'll never think of them that way again."

They watched as the beetle and the larva battled on. The larva dragged the beetle underwater.

Then the beetle reared up and clamped a claw on the larva's head. The larva's tail slapped the water.

With the larva's head in its jaws, the beetle dove underwater. Then it came up again—

at least its rear end did. It spread its wings and folded them as it dove back down.

meep . . . "Diving beetle collecting air under wings," said Thudd. "Like air tank for scuba diver. Can stay underwater lotsa minutes. Maybe hours."

Suddenly Thudd's purple button began to blink. It popped open and a purple beam zoomed out. At the end of the beam appeared a see-through hologram of Uncle Al.

"Hey, guys!" said Uncle Al. "What's with the purple-button emergency? You're supposed to be safe at home."

When Uncle Al visited Andrew and Judy by Hologram Helper, he could hear them but he couldn't see them.

"Hi there, Uncle Al!" said Andrew.

"Hiya, Unkie!" said Thudd.

"You won't believe the trouble we're in!" said Judy.

Uncle Al's fuzzy eyebrows met in the middle of his forehead. "What's going on?" he asked with a frown.

"Um, we're at the pond near the cabin," said Andrew.

"You're at the *pond*!" said Uncle Al. "I told you not to leave the cabin! The pond is an awfully dangerous place for bug-sized kids!"

"We wanted to help you find out why the frogs are disappearing," said Andrew.

"Good golly, Miss Molly!" said Uncle Al. "That's a very brave thing to do, but you should leave that to me.

"I want you to go back to the cabin right now!"

"That'll be hard to do," said Andrew. "The flying machine I invented, the GNAT, got us here. But it sank."

Uncle Al shook his head. "SpongeBob SquarePants on a sugar cookie!" he said. "I'll get there as soon as I can, but it will take a while. The roads are bad here. I had to take a horse trail to this mountain lake."

Andrew nodded. "We'll just hang out on this lily pad till you come get us," he said.

RHUUMMMMM . . . RHUUMMMMM . . . RHUUMMMMM . . .

Uncle Al cocked his head. "I hear frogs,"

he said. "They're bullfrogs, I think."

"Yoop! Yoop! Yoop!" said Thudd.

Uncle Al's eyes grew dark. "Bullfrogs have enormous appetites for, um, insects," he said. "And you guys are the size of—"

Suddenly a huge brownish green lump lunged through the air and plopped down on the lily pad. The lily pad sank, water splashed, and Andrew's stomach flip-flopped as he bounced into the air.

TIME FOR THE SCHNOZZLES

Andrew plopped headfirst into the water.

When he bobbed to the surface, he saw what had tossed him—a bullfrog that was now sitting on a rock.

Andrew squinted at the frog. In its mouth, something was waggling. Andrew heard a faint but familiar scream. Judy!

"Holy moly!" said Andrew.

Eek! squeaked Thudd.

"What can we do?" asked Andrew. "That frog is a thousand times bigger than we are!"

meep . . . "Throw mothballs at frog mouth!" said Thudd.

"I thought mothballs were for bugs and snakes," said Andrew.

meep . . . "Snake got special organ in mouth for smelling," said Thudd. "Frog got same kinda organ. Mothball smell confuse snake. Confuse frog, maybe . . ."

"Judy's got mothballs, too," said Andrew, pulling mothball chips out of his pocket.

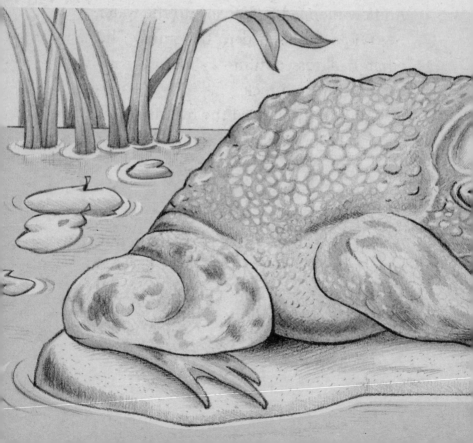

"Judy!" he yelled. "Grab the mothball chips in your pocket. Toss them into the frog's mouth!"

Andrew aimed and threw his mothball chips as hard as he could. Andrew saw Judy shoving something into the frog's mouth.

Suddenly the frog opened its mouth and Judy jumped out.

"Are you okay, Judy?" shouted Andrew.

"I'm covered with frog spit!" she yelled, splashing frantically toward a thick clump of cattails.

The next instant, the bullfrog was zooming over Andrew's head like an airplane!

meep . . . "Bullfrog see something else to eat!" said Thudd.

Andrew swam after Judy toward the cattails.

"The cattails are growing very close together," said Andrew. "They'll keep most things out. We'll be safer in there."

Andrew had just about caught up to Judy. They were swimming through a swarm of whirligig beetles. Each one was spinning like a little top.

Andrew felt a sudden rush of water from below. A splash washed over him. He blinked—and everything went black!

The next thing Andrew knew, he was in

total darkness. His head banged into something hard. *Am I in an underwater cave?* he wondered.

Water was up his nose. He held his breath.

A second later, Andrew felt like someone had shot him out of a water pistol. As he sped along, the water almost dragged his pants off. After a few seconds, he slowed down and paddled quickly to the top.

"Blurf!" he blurted, blowing water from his nose.

"Over here, Bug-Brain!" Judy yelled from close by.

meep . . . "Fish trying to eat whirligig beetles," said Thudd. "Gulp down Drewd and Oody, too."

"It wasn't so bad," said Andrew. "The fish let us go."

meep . . . "Bad! Bad! Bad!" said Thudd. "Cuz fish come back again.

"When fish grab whirligig beetle, beetle

spray nasty stuff. Not taste good.

"Fish spit out beetle. Then fish grab beetle again. Beetle spray again. Fish spit out again. Fish keep catching beetle till beetle got no more nasty stuff to spray. Then fish swallow beetle."

"The fish will come back to get us again when it comes back for the beetles!" said Judy, splashing toward the cattails.

Andrew shook his head. "Maybe not, if we can get away from these whirligig bugs and into the cattails," he said. "But to be safe, we'd better put on the Schnozzles. There's one in the pocket of your Wannabee, Judy."

"Humph," grumped Judy, but she reached into her pocket and pulled out a pair of black goggles with a nose attached and a mustache underneath.

Andrew had invented the Schnozzle to breathe and communicate underwater. The earpieces of the Schnozzles could pick up a person's thoughts and send them to anyone else who was wearing a Schnozzle. It could also send them to Uncle Al's Hologram Helper.

Andrew and Judy shoved their noses into their Schnozzles and stretched the bands over their heads. From one of his pockets, Andrew pulled out two tiny wire spirals and slipped them over Thudd's antennas. With these, Thudd could pick up thoughts from the Schnozzles, too.

Not a moment too soon. In an instant, the fish had gobbled them and a mouthful of whirligig beetles up again. A few seconds later, it spit them out. Then it happened again.

When the fish spit Andrew and Judy out of its mouth this time, the water looked gloomier. And when Andrew looked up, the surface of the water seemed far, far away. They were deeper in the pond now.

That fish will gulp us again before we can get to the top, thought Andrew. *Maybe this time it'll swallow us. We've got to find a place to hide.*

Andrew looked around. A jungle of greenery rose up from below. He spied a tangle of fuzzy-looking plants. Little green bean-shaped sacks bubbled out from their stems.

That looks like a good place to hide, thought Andrew. He dove quickly into the shaggy stems and huddled close to one of the green sacks.

"Noop! Noop! Noop!" squeaked Thudd.

But it was too late. Instantly one of the little bean-shaped sacks popped open. Before Andrew knew it, his top half had been sucked inside!

PLANT FOOD!

Eek! squeaked Thudd. "Drewd inside meat-eating plant! Carnivorous plant! Called bladderwort!

"Stuff inside bladderwort turn Drewd into goo! Then bladderwort absorb Drewd goo!"

"Yowzers!" hollered Andrew, struggling to get himself out. His skin was beginning to itch and tingle. "I think it's starting to eat me!"

Andrew felt something yanking his legs.

Judy was trying to drag him out. But the plant wasn't giving him up.

She let go of Andrew's legs. Through the wall of the sack, Andrew could see Judy like a blurry shadow. She was pulling something from her hair.

Suddenly the sack opened! Andrew pulled himself out.

"What did you *do*?" asked Andrew.

"Used one of my trusty hairpins," said Judy, pushing it back into her hair. "Let's get out of here!"

They swam into a tangle of smooth water-lily stems.

Andrew looked around. "Where's that fish?" he asked.

Judy pointed up. Andrew could see the silvery belly of the fish near the surface. It was eating eggs, the eggs of the yellow-legged frog.

meep . . . "Fish called rainbow trout," said Thudd. "Lotsa years ago, these kindsa fish not live in this pond.

"Few years ago, fisherman put baby trout in pond. Want big trout to catch later. But rainbow trout eat lotsa frog eggs."

"Maybe that's a reason the yellow-legged frogs are disappearing from this pond and others, too," said Andrew.

Judy nodded. "Fishermen stock the ponds with trout," she said. "But they don't realize that the trout will eat up the frog eggs."

"We'll tell Uncle Al," said Andrew.

All around them, strange, shadowy things were swimming, rushing, wriggling—and eating other things.

A tube-shaped creature with long, stringy tentacles was clinging to the water-lily stem beside Andrew.

A tiny creature with fuzzy antennas and one eye in the middle of its head brushed one of the tentacles. In a flash, the tentacle wrapped around the little animal. The other tentacles joined in.

Together, the tentacles stuffed the one-eyed creature into the hole in the middle of the tube-shaped creature.

"Woofers!" said Andrew.

meep . . . "Predator animal called hydra," said Thudd. "Relative of jellyfish.

"When prey animal touch tentacle of hydra, hydra tentacle shoot out stingers. Stingers got hooks to trap prey. Stingers got poison to stun prey. Then tentacles drag prey into stomach to eat."

Just as Andrew was thinking what to do next, a huge bug as long as a pinkie finger swam by. It dashed after a tadpole. Suddenly the front of the bug's face flipped forward! There was a pair of jaws at the end. The jaws caught the tadpole and drew it into its mouth. Then it jetted away.

meep . . . "Dragonfly catch tadpole!" said Thudd.

Judy shook her head. "Dragonflies don't

live underwater, dummy!" she said.

meep . . . "Baby dragonfly," said Thudd. "Called nymph."

"That's no *baby*," said Judy.

meep . . . "Dragonfly nymph *is* baby," insisted Thudd. "Can't lay eggs. Can't make baby dragonflies.

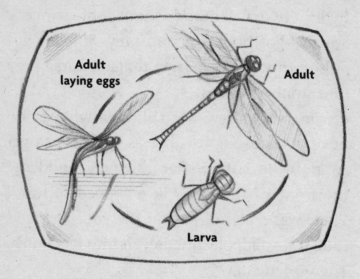

Adult
laying eggs

Adult

Larva

"Nymph live underwater for long time. Maybe seven years.

"Nymph get big, big, big! Shed too-small exoskeleton. Called molting. Grow bigger exoskeleton. This happen lotsa times.

"Then nymph change into adult. Can lay eggs. Have babies.

"Adult dragonfly live short time. Two months, maybe. Enough time to find mate, lay eggs."

Judy shivered and huddled closer to the water-lily stem. "It's not safe on the surface and it's sure not safe down here," she said. "What on earth can we do?"

Andrew looked into the murky water below. He could make out the blurry outlines of plants and rocks.

"Let's go to the bottom of the pond," he said. "We can hide under a rock until Uncle Al comes to get us."

"Cheese Louise!" said Judy. "Who knows what's down there. It could be *worse!*"

Andrew spied a huge, ghostly-looking larva perched on a nearby water-lily stem. It was perfectly still.

As Andrew looked more closely, he could

see that it wasn't a live larva at all. It was just an empty shell.

"Wowzers!" said Andrew. "There's a giant bug skeleton with nobody in it!"

meep . . . "Exoskeleton of water tiger," said Thudd.

"Super-duper pooper-scooper!" said Andrew. "It's really scary-looking. We can get inside and camouflage ourselves."

They swam over to it. The exoskeleton was clear and felt like plastic. Andrew and Judy crept under it. They jiggled it to loosen it from the stem and balanced it on their heads. It was very light. Looking through the skeleton made things a little blurry, like looking through someone else's glasses.

Disguised as a fearsome water tiger, they crept down the water-lily stem, deeper into the pond.

THUDD

THE MYSTERY OF TOO MANY LEGS

"Look!" said Judy, pausing on the water-lily stem. She lifted the exoskeleton to get a better look. "Tadpoles with legs!"

"Wowzers schnauzers!" said Andrew. "They've all got tails, but some of them have just hind legs. And some of them have all four legs."

meep . . . "Few weeks after tadpole hatch from egg, hind legs begin to grow," said Thudd. "Later, front legs grow under skin, pop through skin. Then tail begin to go away. Tadpole stop eating. Body turn tail into energy to use as food."

"What's *that*?" asked Judy, pointing ahead.

Through the murky water and blurry skeleton, it looked like two long, thin tree trunks were coming toward them.

meep . . . "Legs of big bird," said Thudd. "Legs of heron. Heron eat lotsa fish.

"But heron do favor for fish, too. Fish eggs stick to feet of heron. When heron fly to other pond or lake, carry fish eggs to new place."

Judy shrugged. "As long as the heron isn't interested in bug-sized things," she said.

"Woofers!" said Andrew, slipping down. He struggled to keep the exoskeleton over him and Judy and still hang on. "This stem is so slimy!"

meep . . . "Stem covered with algae," said Thudd. "Tiny plants. Too small to see with eyes.

"Algae not got leaves. Not got roots. But algae use energy from sun to make food. Same as other plants. Algae make water look green. Lotsa animals eat algae."

Thudd pointed to a lump that was crawling up another stem. "Snail eat algae," said Thudd. "Snail scrape off algae with thousands, thousands of tiny teeth."

The water swarmed with swimmers—insects and wormy things and tadpoles and frogs.

A long, flat, ribbon-like creature swam so close that it almost knocked Andrew and Judy's exoskeleton off the lily stem.

"Cheese Louise!" said Judy. "What was *that*?"

meep . . . "Leech," said Thudd.

The leech caught up with a small fish. It wrapped itself around the fish and held it tight.

meep . . . "Leech sucking blood from fish," said Thudd. "When leech drink enough blood, leech let fish go."

"Eeeeuw!" Judy shivered, pushing Andrew to move faster down the stem. "Leeches are vampires!"

"Yoop! Yoop! Yoop!" said Thudd. "Leech saliva got special stuff to make bite not hurt while leech suck blood. Sometime big animal not know that leech biting.

"Leech saliva got stuff to make blood flow fast."

Suddenly frogs, lots of them, sped by their exoskeleton.

"Holy moly!" said Andrew, lifting the skeleton for a better view. "There's a frog with *six legs*!"

"And there's one with just *three legs*!" said Judy.

meep . . . "Short time ago, kids in Minnesota visit pond. Find lotsa frogs with lotsa problems. Some got too many legs. Some got no back legs. Some got just one eye.

"Kids tell whole world that frogs got problems. Scientists investigate."

"Why are bad things happening to the frogs?" asked Andrew.

meep . . . "No one know for sure," said Thudd. "Could be lotsa things.

"Could be kinda light from sun. Ultraviolet light hurt frog eggs. More ultraviolet light come from sun now.

"Could be stuff that people use to kill

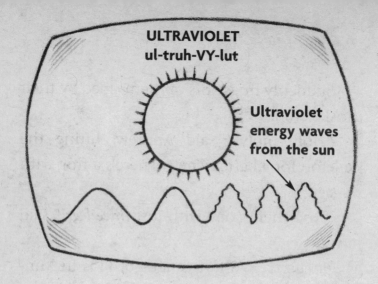

ULTRAVIOLET
ul-truh-VY-lut

Ultraviolet energy waves from the sun

bugs. Bug killers get into water. Frogs live in water. Breathe through skin. Bug killers get into frogs through skin. Do bad things, maybe.

"Animals called parasites live in water, too. Parasites gotta use other animals to live, to make babies.

"Some kindsa parasite burrow into back end of tadpoles. Mess up place where frog legs grow. Make frog grow more legs sometimes. Sometimes no legs."

"The poor frogs!" said Judy.

meep . . . "Frog with leg problems have hard time catching food," said Thudd. "Easy for predator to catch, too."

"We'll tell Uncle Al about all this," said Andrew as they crept carefully down the lily stem. "Maybe we can help save the frogs."

"Humph," grumped Judy. "We can't even figure out how to save ourselves. This is all your fault, Bug-Brain!"

Through the cloudy water, Andrew could see rocks at the bottom of the pond.

"There must be some rocks that don't have anything nasty living under them," he said.

Judy rolled her eyes. "And the way we can tell is by whether or not we get eaten," she said. "Nice!"

Andrew and Judy were half an inch from the bottom of the pond now. Suddenly the exoskeleton whacked Andrew on the side of his head. And then it zoomed off!

Andrew watched another water tiger speeding away with their camouflage!

"Cheese Louise!" hollered Judy as they touched down in the squishy mud. "We've got nothing to protect us!"

"We can hide under that giant rock ahead," said Andrew. "It's so big, it will be easy for Uncle Al to find it."

They tried to hurry. It wasn't easy to do underwater. With every step, their tiny feet stirred up little swirls of muck.

As they were passing by a clam-like crea-ture buried in the mud, they saw that a small fish seemed to be struggling at the edge of it.

"That poor little fish is stuck," said Judy. "Let's help it."

"Noop! Noop! Noop!" said Thudd. "Not real fish!"

BAD STUFF AT THE BOTTOM

Just then, a big fish darted toward the little fish at the edge of the shell and bit it.

A cloud of tiny dark specks puffed out of the shell. The specks rained down on Andrew and Judy and the big fish. The big fish backed off and swam away.

Andrew and Judy shook off the specks. They looked like teeny clams with hooks.

meep . . . "Big shell buried in mud belong to animal called mussel," said Thudd. "Mussel got strange life cycle. Mussel larva got hooks. Hook on to gills of fish. Suck blood from fish for a while. Then drop off.

"To get fish to come close, mussel got lure that look like little fish. When real fish come to bite fake fish, mussel shoot larva at fish. Mussel make millions and millions of larva babies."

"Wowzers schnauzers!" said Andrew. "That's *amazing*!"

Andrew and Judy kept shuffling through the silky mud and tangled stems.

Andrew tripped over a twig. But as he got up, he saw it wasn't a twig. It was a tube made of grains of sand and tiny pebbles. It was moving and something was sticking out of one end of it.

meep . . . "Caddis-fly larva," said Thudd. "Larva make silk. Use silk like glue. Stick stuff together. Make case to hide in."

"There are a lot of these cases," said Andrew. "Some of them are empty."

meep . . . "When caddis-fly larva grow, leave old case," said Thudd. "Make bigger case to move into.

"Later, caddis-fly larva turn into flying bug."

"Cheese Louise!" said Judy. "A lot of bugs start out not looking like bugs at all! And they spend most of their stupid lives in the water!"

"Yoop! Yoop! Yoop!" said Thudd. "But bugs not so stupid. Bugs been living on earth longer than any other animals. More kindsa bugs than any other animals. Many million times more bugs on earth than humans."

Suddenly a large, flat, round shape tumbled through the water and landed a few inches away from Andrew and Judy. Then another plopped down closer.

"We're getting bombed!" yelled Judy.

A dark, oval shape scooted sideways and buried itself in the mucky bottom.

"Hmmmm . . . ," said Andrew. "This reminds me of something. . . ."

Judy kicked Andrew's leg. "Move it!" she said. "Before we get smooshed."

"I've got it!" said Andrew. "People are skipping stones up there! If we get back to the surface fast, we can find them!"

"Noooo!" said Judy, bounding toward the big rock. "We've gotta wait till the stones stop falling. We could get crushed."

She arrived at the rock and quickly scooped muck from under it. Then she squeezed herself into the hiding place. Andrew wiggled in beside her.

"Stop shoving me," said Judy.

"I'm not shoving you," said Andrew.

"Yes you *are*," said Judy.

"No I'm *not*," said Andrew. "*You're* shoving *me*."

Andrew reached over to touch what was nudging him. He felt something cold and hard and sharp. A shiver ran down his spine.

SUPER-DUPER POOPER-SCOOPER!

"Let's get out of here, Judy!" he said. *"Now!"*

They scrambled out. Andrew felt something scraping the rear of his Wannabee pants.

Andrew turned and squinted. Through the murk, he glimpsed one of the scariest things he had ever seen.

It was a huge, dark head with wide-open jaws that looked like giant pliers. Long legs with claws at their tips jutted from its centipede-like body.

Eek! "Hellgrammite!" squeaked Thudd. "Larva of big, big fly."

Andrew spied one of the skipping stones and started paddling toward it. "Let's hide under that pebble, Judy!" he said. "It's our only chance!"

As they buried themselves under the pebble, the hellgrammite reared up. Its jaws stabbed at a caddis-fly larva inside its case. The hellgrammite crushed the case, dragged out the larva, and stuffed it between its twitching jaws.

"How will we ever get out of here alive?" asked Judy.

Andrew scratched behind one of his antennas. He reached into a pocket and pulled out a tiny cube wrapped in white paper. Blue letters on the wrapper spelled out UMBUBBLE.

Andrew had invented the Umbubble as a way for Judy and him to protect themselves if they were caught in a watery environment. The Umbubble had worked very well when they were flushed down the toilet.

Andrew unwrapped the cube, crammed it

into his mouth, and chewed. Then he tried to blow it up like bubble gum. But it was much harder to blow the Umbubble up in water than in air. Andrew huffed and puffed. The Umbubble blew up to the size of Andrew's tiny nose. Then it blew up to the size of his little head. But Andrew couldn't get it any bigger.

"Help me blow up the Umbubble, Judy," said Andrew.

"Eeeeuw!" complained Judy. "I'm not putting my mouth on anything you've had in *your* mouth!"

Andrew cocked his head. "Would you rather be a hellgrammite snack?" he asked.

Judy rolled her eyes, chomped down on the Umbubble, and they both began to blow.

The Umbubble started to puff up. Suddenly it was as big as a Ping-Pong ball. When Andrew and Judy stopped for a breath, it sucked them both inside!

The Umbubble slowly rose up through the green pond. It passed fish and tadpoles and bristly bugs chasing prickly bugs. *I hope the Umbubble doesn't look tasty,* thought Andrew.

A few seconds later, they popped to the surface. The sun had disappeared behind dark, fast-moving clouds.

Putt putt putt putt putt . . .

VRRRROOOOOOM!

Through the pale blue wall of the Umbubble, Andrew could see boats on the water—toy boats. There was a tugboat, a speedboat, and a big sailboat—with a helicopter on the back deck.

"People!" yelled Judy, pointing toward the shore.

On the edge of the pond, four kids about Andrew's age were laughing and using remote controls to guide the boats.

A boy with curly red hair was skipping stones.

"If only we could get on one of those boats," said Judy. "But they're moving so fast."

"Wait a minute!" said Andrew. "I still have the remote from the GNAT. It works on all kinds of things. Maybe it will work on these boats—*or the helicopter!*"

Andrew pointed the remote at the helicopter and clicked. The rotor at the top started to turn, slowly at first, then faster and faster, till it was almost invisible.

Andrew pressed the controls. The helicopter lifted off the deck of the sailboat.

"What *is* that?" came a voice from the edge of the pond.

"It's the helicopter!" came another voice. "It took off by itself!"

Andrew steered the helicopter toward the Umbubble and guided it down till it touched the water.

"Do you think it's gonna sink?" said someone on the shore.

Andrew and Judy punched their way out of the Umbubble and paddled to the helicopter. They climbed in through the open window.

It was only mid-afternoon, but the sky was getting dark fast. Fat raindrops began to pelt the water. Water splashed into the helicopter's cabin.

Using his remote, Andrew made the helicopter lift into the air.

"Woofers!" he cried. They were flying!

Even though it was raining hard now, the kids on the edge of the pond stood perfectly still. All eyes were on the helicopter.

"It's coming this way!" said a tall, dark-haired girl.

"It's like there's a pilot!" said a short boy with a high voice.

The next instant, the sky exploded with light.

ZAAAAPPPP!

Andrew tingled all over. Suddenly he felt like he was being shot out of a cannon! Then everything went black.

"YEEOUCH!" Andrew hollered. A terrible

pain shot through his butt. His hands touched something hard below him. He had slammed down on a rock at the edge of the pond.

The kids he had seen on the shore were standing over him. Their mouths were open so wide, they could have swallowed tennis balls.

"Hoooeee!" said the red-haired boy. "You guys got hit by lightning!"

"Ooooooooh . . ." It was Judy, groaning. She was leaning on her elbows in a patch of nearby cattails. And she was the size she used to be when she was a regular thirteen-year-old girl!

Andrew's eyes grew wide as he looked at his legs and his hands and his arms. They were the size they used to be when he was a regular ten-year-old boy! "Super-duper pooper-scooper!" shouted Andrew.

Next to his right hand was the tiny little rotor from the top of the helicopter.

The sky was a lighter shade of gray now and the rain had stopped. "Looks like the storm is over," said Andrew to the kids standing over him.

"You were out for five minutes from the time you crashed," said the dark-haired girl. "You were about the size of a peach pit when the helicopter cracked open, and you kept growing like a crazy weed."

Andrew heard the sound of bushes rustling. He looked up to see the head of a tall man with shaggy hair bobbing up behind the kids.

"Uncle Al!" shouted Andrew.

"Hiya, Unkie!" squeaked Thudd.

"What took you so long?" asked Judy.

"Christopher Columbus on a Krispy Kreme doughnut!" gasped Uncle Al. "You're back to normal size!"

"They were cuter when they were tiny," said the dark-haired girl.

Uncle Al introduced himself to the kids. "I'm Andrew and Judy's uncle," he said.

He shook his head and smiled at Andrew and Judy. "How on earth did you get un-shrunk?" he asked.

The kids began to speak at once.

"They got hit by lightning!"

"They took off from the pond in a toy helicopter!"

"The helicopter crashed on the shore," said the dark-haired girl. "They were teeny-tiny for a minute, then they started to get big—fast!"

"It was so cool!" said the red-haired boy. "Like those little toys you put in water and they grow!"

"The lightning got us big again," said Andrew. "It was the electricity."

"I feel like Frankenstein," said Judy.

Andrew chuckled. "You *look* like—"

"Andrew!" interrupted Uncle Al with a twinkle in his eyes. "Act your size!"

Andrew laughed. "We sure have a lot to tell you about frogs!" he said.

"Great!" said Uncle Al. "Let's discuss it over a pepperoni pizza. Who wants to come?"

"Super-duper pooper-scooper!" said Andrew. "I'm starving."

"Me too!" said the short boy with the high voice.

"Hot doggies!" said the red-haired boy. "Let's go!"

"Can we have mushrooms?" asked the dark-haired girl.

"I want mushrooms, too!" Judy chimed in. "And sausage!"

meep . . . "Everything okey-dokey now!" said Thudd.

THUDD

TRUE STUFF

Thudd wanted to tell you more about frogs, floating brains, and other weird pond stuff, but he was too busy saving Andrew and Judy from hungry spiders and water tigers. Here's what he wanted to say:

• When cold winters come, some frogs do more than hibernate—they actually freeze solid! Their hearts stop beating, their brains stop working, and their eyes turn white! When the weather gets warmer, the ice in the frog's body begins to melt. In a few hours, the frog comes to life again.

   Scientists are trying to figure out how

frogs can freeze, shut down their organs, and still survive. It may be because the ice forms outside their cells but not inside.

When water freezes, it expands. If the water inside tiny, delicate cells froze, it would rip the cells apart. The water inside these frogs' cells has an "anti-freeze" made of a kind of sugar!

• When a frog swallows a meal, its eyes close and its eyeballs go down into its head! Frogs use their eyeballs to help push food down their throats!

• The biggest frog in the world lives in Africa, is a foot long (not including its legs), and can weigh more than seven pounds. The world's smallest frog would barely cover your pinkie fingernail!

• When a frog eats something that could make it sick, it throws up. But it doesn't just throw up the bad food, it throws up its whole stomach! While its stomach is hanging outside its mouth, the frog uses its front legs to clean the stomach off—then swallows it to get it back down!

• In China, people munch fried water beetles as snacks! (Dee-lish! They taste kind of like chips.) In Thailand, water beetles are ground up and turned into a tasty sauce.

• As insects grow, they go through a process called metamorphosis, a word that means "changing form."

Most insects hatch from eggs as worm-like creatures. As they get bigger, they break out of their exoskeletons. In the final stage before becoming an adult, many insects make a hard case, called a pupa, around themselves for protection. Inside the pupa, they destroy most of their bodies with digestive juices. From the cells that are left, a new body grows in a whole new shape. That's why a butterfly looks so different from a caterpillar.

• Have you ever noticed that many fish have

dark backs and silvery bellies? That's an example of camouflage! To a predator looking down from above, the water looks dark. The dark color of a fish's back makes it hard to see. To an underwater predator looking up, the surface of the water looks bright. The light color of a fish's belly makes it harder to see from below.

• Lightning is extremely dangerous. You should go inside as soon as you know a storm is coming or if you hear thunder, even if you don't see lightning. Lightning tends to strike tall things, so never hide under a tree.

If you get caught in an open space when lightning is near, never lie down on the ground. Protect yourself with the "lightning crouch." It's a little hard to do, so practice the crouch before you need it.

Crouch and balance yourself on your toes. Super important: MAKE SURE YOUR HEELS ARE TOUCHING EACH OTHER! If lightning strikes nearby, electricity will travel up the nearest foot. If your heels are touching, it will travel to the other heel and back down into the ground again. This will keep electricity from damaging the rest of your body. Stay safe!

THUDD

WHERE TO FIND MORE TRUE STUFF

Want to know more about the weird things that go on in peaceful-looking ponds? Read these!

• *One Small Square: Pond* by Donald M. Silver (New York: Learning Triangle Press, 1994). Take this book with you to a pond. It will help you to discover and understand the amazing plants and creatures that live in all parts of the pond. You'll also learn how things change through the day and the seasons.

• *Eyewitness: Pond & River* (New York: DK Publishing, 2005). This book, with its great pictures, is like a visit to a pond.

• *Song of the Water Boatman & Other Pond Poems* by Joyce Sidman (Boston: Houghton Mifflin, 2005). A fun combination of poems and science about pond creatures.

• *Uncover a Frog* by Aimee Bakken (San Diego: Silver Dolphin Books, 2006). Want to see what goes on inside a frog without taking one apart? Then this book is for you!

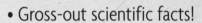
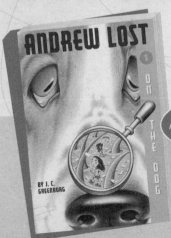

Bring magic into your life with these enchanting books!

Magic Tree House® series
by Mary Pope Osborne

The Magic Elements Quartet
by Mallory Loehr
Water Wishes
Earth Magic
Wind Spell
Fire Dreams

Dragons
by Lucille Recht Penner

Fox Eyes
by Mordicai Gerstein

King Arthur's Courage
by Stephanie Spinner

The Magic of Merlin
by Stephanie Spinner

Unicorns
by Lucille Recht Penner

ABOUT THE ILLUSTRATOR

JAN GERARDI has illustrated many books for children. She is also an art director and a graphic designer. She lives in New Jersey with her husband and daughter and three dogs.